WHAT I LIKE

Catherine and Laurence Anholt

WALKER BOOKS

AND SUBSIDIARIES

LONDON • BOSTON • SYDNEY

What I like is...

1. This book may be kept three weeks.
    It is to be returned on / before the last date
    stamped below.
2. A fine of 20p will be charged for every week
    or part of week a book is overdue.

For Maria and Joe

First published 1991 by
Walker Books Ltd
87 Vauxhall Walk
London SE11 5HJ

This edition published 1998

2 4 6 8 10 9 7 5 3 1

Printed in Hong Kong

British Library Cataloguing in Publication Data
A catalogue record for this book is
available from the British Library.

ISBN 0-7445-6189-2 (Hbk)
ISBN 0-7445-6070-5 (Pbk)

time to play

a holiday

toys

(some) boys

waking early

hair all curly

What we like is…

jumping about

having a shout

going out

I don't like…

getting lost

I love…

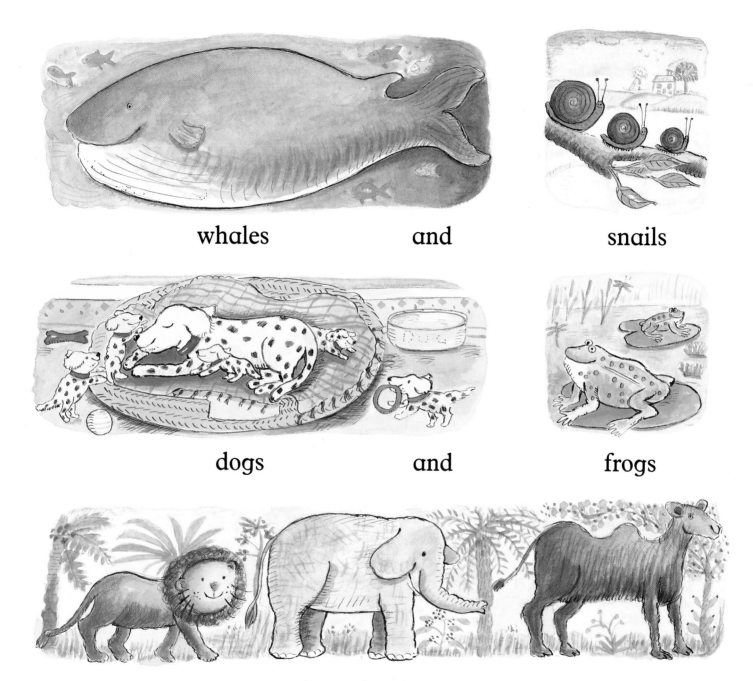

whales   and   snails

dogs   and   frogs

lots of animals

Sometimes
we don't like…

being a pair

people who stare

having to share

I hate…

thunder and lightning

I like...

playing with my mother

and my new baby brother

What I like is...

ice-cream

a funny dream

my thermos flask

my monster mask

I love…

playing the fool   a swimming pool   nursery school

I don't like...

fleas

peas

bees

aches

snakes

breaks

bumps

lumps

dumps

rats

gnats

bats

What we all like is...

a Christmas tree

watching TV

a place to hide

a pony ride

let's pretend

a happy end and . . .

Making a friend.